The *Quirky* Feminine 2.0

Sudeshna Chakrabarti

First Published in December 2021

ISBN: 978-93-5472-745-0

BLUEROSE PUBLISHERS

www.bluerosepublishers.com

info@bluerosepublishers.com

+91 8882 898 898

Cover Design:

Muskan Sachdeva

Typographic Design:

Namrata Saini

Distributed by: BlueRose, Amazon, Flipkart, Shopclues

Dedication

Dedicated to all the women throughout the world, who have accepted themselves as they are

Preface

My inspiration has been my father "Chirantan Chakrabarti" who is my mentor and helps me in understanding my truest ability with every passing day.

My mother "Meenakshi Chakrabarti" a goddess in her true nature has been an inspiration to me through her intellect, beauty and fiery personality. As I grew up she had made me understand the deeper meanings of the ritualistic process performed during Kali and Durga puja. This made me understand the true inner goddess that lay deeply embedded within each woman which when invoked could fight their inner and external demons in true divine timing.

Acknowledgment

I would like to thank my bestest friend Neil 'D' Souza for motivating me throughout the project.

My special heartfelt thanks to Fayaz, Bhaanupriya and the team at Blue Rose Publishers who have helped me on various stages of the draft of the book.

Last, not the least............ I want to thank the feminine supremacy, Goddess Durga to provide me with faith and courage to pen down my oratory thoughts into a written one.

Contents

Subarnalata

It was 5:55 am in the morning and Calcutta had already started to prepare itself for morning routine. The chirping sounds of the birds and the splashing of water near the Ganges ghats could be heard all over the metropolis. The city was slowly waking upto the human disruptions. The blaring sounds of the traffic, the irritating uncanny vendor calls and the regular tap water fights between Bimala and Nirmala mashi were all playing their part by contributing to the cacophony. Amidst this chaos, Subarnalata was in a deep slumber thinking about the sumptuous breakfast she would be devouring in the morning along with Taaru da.

In her dream-Taaru da was her hero. Unlike the six packed hero archetype who usually comes in every girl's dream and fills the void in their life with candypop fantasies. Taaru da, resembled the lankier version of a south Indian hero who was the local chaiwalla and his weapon of desire was the unclean reused oil filled utensil. This utensil was an elixir to Subarnalata. Very often, in her own dreams, she would appear wearing her favorite red kurti from Dakshinapan, with her jet-black hair glistening against the north Kolkata sun as she slowly walked towards him. Upon seeing Subarnalata a wide smile would appear on his lips whilst the 90's song "*Chaandni*" would be playing in the background from the age-old radio which belonged to his father. The smile was generally suppressed due to his shop being on the main road. The pollution emitted by those local buses and the noise generated by the potbellied bus conductor along with complaints from his overweight cranky wife only led to a severe headache. Subarnalata was different, she never unloaded her problems onto him or discussed anything with any of her friends or colleagues in the chai stall, she often came alone with a book which was tucked tightly tucked under her arm. She devoured that enormous aloo filled samosa with cauliflower while simultaneously being hypnotized by his appeal and charm. Leave alone the chai which was like elixir and him being Mohini of heavens serving it, it was her ritualistic offering to Taaru da before she started to read any book as it made her oblivious to the unruly surroundings.

Subarnalata was a Bengali who was born and bred in Calcutta. She resided in one of those typical red and green buildings of North Kolkata near the famous college street. College Street was famous for its lanes filled with secondhand book shops and coffee shops which served Subarnalata famous egg sandwich The stacked books in every shop welcomed her with open arms and reminded her that loyalty still existed even during this kalyuga. She was studying economics in one of the most prestigious colleges of Calcutta. She loved her numbers and the fact that the subject was applicable in real life. This made her analyze economic various situations from a different perspective. Apart from attempting to understand Karl Marx theory or any other articles written by a top economist, Subaranalata was also fixated on understanding the simplified meanings behind the complicated yet beautiful Sanskrit language which was woven into Hindu mythology. She was awed by her mother's dedication towards the gods and goddesses, However, what fascinated her the most was the unshakeable faith her mother retained despite of the traumatic experiences which had occurred in her life. Like any mother, she was a divine goddess to Subarnalata and the fulcrum of her life who had not only given her birth but had also changed her life in many definite ways. However, both were oblivious to the fact that their individual contribution would positively impact the society in the upcoming days.

It was Friday and the weekends were loaded with household chores and silly homework. Subaranalata sat appalled. She believed homework was nothing but a hinderance in her time of reading Relishing in the glory of doing well in school, she sidelined the notion of homework altogether.

She entered her home and was welcomed by the smell of jasmine emanating from the incense sticks, lit by her mother Ashapurna devi. Her mother looked like a divine goddess, wearing the white saree embellished with a red and gold border. Her long wet hair due to untimely bath taken for the evening puja made her look fresh. There was something ethereal about her energy too. Subarnalata stood in the hallway struck by her mother's divine energy. It only dawned upon her a few minutes later that she was looking like a fool when she saw a mouse peeving from a small hole on the wall that made a demarcation between the hallway and the kitchen, it was waiting for her to move so it could scamper across the hallway. Subarnalata made a move towards the kitchen and one by one started to unload the groceries that she had gotten from the local bazaar which according to the entire locality was more trustworthy than the high-end products they sold in the new age malls. "*Ami eshe gechi Ma,*" (*I have come back*) Subarnalata announced with a tired voice. As she looked up, she realized her mother already had a tray filled with hot snacks and ginger tea which immediately dilated Subarnalata's pupils, "How did you know Maa? "Stuttered Subarnalata

"Ami *Ma, shob jani,*" (*Iam a mother , I know everything*) Subarnalata devoured the snacks and gulped down the tea She was desperately waiting to retire to her room, freshen up and finally finish the economic theory that she had started a week ago. However, she was finding it difficult to complete it due to several distractions. She was about to get up when she heard her father enter the living room. Immediately, she could smell the stench of alcohol which soon replaced the Jasmine fragrance that had filled her nostrils. This caused her immense anger because it made her feel that someone had disrespected her mother's hard work. Subarnalata's father was a renowned advocate who was famous for his strings of successful cases which often appeared in the local newspaper. This led to the swelling of his bank accounts and his tummy' the latter filled by greed and alcohol. Her father' success had gotten to his head and this drastic change had left her mother and she in a state of despair. This required involvement with elite upper classes and overindulgence in alcoholic drinks as well as unnecessary under table bribe. He would often come home drunk and sing English songs, describing the glamour of the parties he had attended. He also started to find her mother "gaiyya"(*backward*) and this disrespectfulness led to a lot of pent up anger inside of Subaranalata. She would get further aggrieved due to the lack of retaliation and response from her mother. Even though Subaranalata was tired, her over protectiveness toward her mother suddenly filled her body with a splurge of energy. "*Ei toh Jibon*" her father started singing and Subarnalata started rolling her eyes at the poor choice of song, "At least, he could have chosen Elvis Presley ", she muttered under her breath. Suddenly she heard a mocking laugh coming from the hallway, and she rushed to her mothers' rescue only to see her father wearing a shirt pant which was newly bought for his sudden glamour parties which were now the center of his universe. He was leaning on to her mother's shoulder putting all his weight on her fragile shoulder. This enraged Subarnalata further. "You see," he stammered, "You are the wife of the Calcutta's Top Advocate. You need to level up and start wearing those English dresses and not these *gaiyya* drapes." Ashapurna devi was literally limping to help her husband towards the bedroom, despite her fragile body in pain. Subarnalata was now clenching her teeth, but her consciousness kept reminding her that it was her own biological father. Her mother threw her a calming look which just reminded Subaranalata that her mother could handle it all. She just sighed and left to retire towards her room to complete her checklist of the day. That night she added extra cinnamon to her warm milk to make her sleep peacefully.

Next morning, Subarnalata woke up at 9:00 am. Saturday and Sundays were always pleasurable. Due to the abundance of time in their hand. Usually her mother would prepare the most sumptuous breakfast in the world (Taaru da comes second of course) which included loochi aloo dum (famous *Bengali vegetarian dishes which made all the non-vegetarian dishes appear less macho*) and the pistachio kheer, with karuna mashi (the notorious in house maid known for being a kleptomaniac) she tossed and turned in her bed making the side table shiver vehemently as the calendar toppled over her diary due to her ministrations. The table calendar showcased the dates of the year 2015, but it was very special to her. It was gifted by her late grandmother, the last gift given by her. It contained unique and novel pictures which were not found easily in the market. It also included all the pictures of Mahavidya forms of goddess Parvati- a concept very few could behold & was one of the most appealing forms of the divine goddess. She was one of the calmest and collected forms of Parvati goddess who knew the seen and the unseen. But, most importantly, she was the reasoning factor behind all the cosmic events which was leading to the infinite abundance. Only a spiritually awakened mind would understand. She was lost in her trail of thoughts when a shrill voice disrupted the peaceful environment rendering everyone in the household in a state of panic. It seemed that the shrill voice had emanated from the Mukherjee residence, their frequents fights in the household was about to be the talk of the entire North Kolkata. Mr Mukherjee was a typical chauvinistic man who believed the son should be carrying the weight of the legacy entirely on his shoulders. However, it was his daughter *Chinnmaya* who was the bright star in the household, she had not only been offered double promotion in her school twice but her innate ability to solve mathematical problems at the tip of her tongue had astonished many learned teachers and scholars alike. The fights in the Mukherjee household revolved around the money, where the man of the household would rather invest in his son than his own daughter. Mom had gone to pacify Sheena, with a glass of water to prevent her blood pressure from escalating further. Sheena always believed in the potential of her daughter. She also thought that success of her daughter could compensate for the sacrifices she had made and the humiliation she had faced from her husband and society for being a seventh standard pass. Subarnalata decided to teach guide *Chinnmaya* and provided her with tuition which would help in polishing her skills further.

That weekend she found her father rather quiet, listening to songs of Rabindranath and often, glancing at her mother like a guilty eyed cat. This strengthened her suspicion further of him indulging in some forbidden pleasure. In the upcoming few months, she found herself submerged in preparation for college exams, providing *Chinmaya* and her best friend tuition and researching for the right college for her further studies. One of the major factors of her submerging in work was her suspicion related to her father's awkward behavior towards them. In the evening he would often bring the infamous *nolengurer sondesh* of Bengal along with hot snacks, on someday it was accompanied with expensive perfume and those modern silk sarees, and it's seemed that his intoxication had been on a temporary holiday. Subarnalata's concern was not directed towards her father's changed behavior which seemed comical and foolish to the intelligent eyes, but it seemed that his hush hush conversations with the driver had increased, and she found him secretly hiding some things in the back of the car.

Although, Subarnalata was an intelligent person, she wanted to avoid donning the Byomkesh Bakshi hat. She would often indulge in intimate conversations with Taarru da who seemed to have provided her relaxation with his sweat infused samosa and tobacco-stained smile. Calcutta seemed bearable with his smile and the age-old radio which produced some of the best Sridevi songs. It seemed they were dedicated to her. Often, her mind would wander on how she would look in those multicolored chiffon sarees with Taaru da running in his white sweater on the snow-clad mountain tops with the rusty steel kettle and she would melt into his arms. The vendor selling flowers suddenly disrupted her thoughts, who seemed to have enjoyed the fatal attraction between Taaru da and her. He was seemingly very happy to intrude in that private space with a mischievous smile and *rajnigandha* (flower) , with a heavy sigh she bought a couple of string of flowers and offered one of those to Taaru da who had instead, decided to make it an ornament on his overweight wife's hair bun to calm her down.This was not a betrayal to Subaranalata but to let her know she had a special position in their life.

Whilst she returned home, she found her mouse waiting for her to scamper along the room, which had almost become a ritual for the animal and a stale game for Subarnalata. She put the flowers in the *thaakur ghar* (temple *of the house*), she found a hallmark card and a box of sweets, along with a friendship band on top of the dining table. It appeared that Chinnmaya not only topped her school semester but had also been able to impress some of the external teachers from reputed colleges across India. They wanted her to enroll in their colleges with a full scholarship. Chinnmaya's mother decided to throw a farewell party and wanted to shower Subarnalata with praises, sweets, possibly honey. Basically, she had to be the Sivalinga on *Shivratri(the linga statue of deity Shiva was worshipped on the auspicious occasion of Shivratri)* where all forms of sweets was to be showered upon by the coming ladies of all ages, shapes and sizes.

It was the month of August, and the citizens of Calcutta were perspiring along with other cities across India. However, Subaranalata's mind was wandering on her examinations results. She had just finished college and was deciding upon her future master's degree while simultaneously thinking about her final year examination results. In just one week and she would be entering a new chapter of her life. The party at *Chinmmayas* house was filled with balloons, streamers, cake from Flury's and some of the rhyme songs. The aunties found it an opportunity to giggle,gossip and play Chinese whisper on "Who *is doing what in the society*"

Subarnalata started yawning and thanked her stars for once that her mother Ashapurna devi was made of different material. She would rather be helping Sheena organized the party and extend a helping hand. Chinmaya happily introduced some of her best friends chinky, minky and shanky to Subarnalata with a swelling pride by calling her *didi* of the century (seldom did she knew that another was in the making). They even gave her a pink colored birthday cap to which she happily obliged and started playing *ringa ringa* roses but for once found it light heartening.

She returned home with boxes of sweets and snacks of all sorts;a streamer stuck to her dress along with cotton candy bits and she found herself swaying to the music. Suddenly it dawned upon her that her mother was silent and never had an opportunity to spend time with her mother alone. This was indeed a great opportunity given that the house was a few steps away. She finally asked her mom "How are you, Mom?" upon which her mother's eyes widened and stared at her longingly, "I have not heard that in a while."

"Why are you so quiet Ma?" as I started tugging at her saree and rested my head on her arms.

"Your father is having an illicit affair," she replied calmly. This sentence shook me from inside and I abruptly stopped in my tracks.

"What?!" I blabbered unintelligently. My mother didn't reply she just took my hand nonchalantly and rubbed the palms of my hand in a soothing manner.

After a while she spoke, "This is not his first time. Honestly, at the beginning, I was torn apart too but now I'm very much oblivious to this fact and have devoted myself completely to God. When I look at you, it seems God had rewarded me with so many blessings. I cannot fathom to leave him and remarry someone else, you are the mark of my achievement," she paused for a while and looked at me with tears glistening in her eyes, "Look at what you have become I'm so proud of you Subarnalata. I just want you to always remember, you are the priority in my life, and you should always put yourself first."

As they entered their home, her mother glanced at her lovingly and said "Don't discuss this with your father. He is your father after all and whatever you say or do would not erase the hurt, he has caused me." Subarnalata was left speechless. The only numbness she found was cinnamon milk and cardamom on the rocks consoled by some Geeta Dutta songs.

In the upcoming weeks, Subaranalata avoided her father as much as possible. The household seemed to be running normally, despite the heavy baggage she was carrying in her heart. Next morning, Mr Dutta called Subarnalata in his staff room, she was quite nervous.

Despite being a teacher's pet, she often got cold feet. Mr Dutta was very happy with her examination results and wanted her to pursue her master's in economics in the leading college of Calcutta. He planned on introducing her to Mr Chatterjee- one of the leading economists of India. He had written several research books and students from around the world had successfully completed their PhD Degree whilst producing some of the most eminent economic research papers.

Subarnalata was in seventh heaven and this time while entering the house, she was found herself beaming with joy and chasing the mouse and not allowing it to scamper back to its hole. This behavior lead Karuna mashi to believe that some type of spirit had possessed her and quickly went to grab the broom when suddenly Subarnalata started chasing Karunamashi out of fun. This led to Karuna mashi panting and almost dropping at ashapurna devis feet and while Subaranalata followed her with a wicked smile.

Upon giving her mother the news, her mother ran to a temple house and started chanting the hymns to which Subaranalata was a bit taken aback. Her mother's running was quite like those 90's heroine in the movies and the filmy run almost seemed silly yet quirky.

That night Subarnalata thought that she had finally achieved bliss without the cinnamon milk.

The loud noises that were originating from her parent's room had woken her up from the deep sleep. She could hear a woman thundering or roaring like a Royal Bengal tiger which almost made Subarnalata slipped down the staircase. She had never seen her mother in such an avatar before. She was screaming at the top her lungs at her father. While he remained shell shocked and stood in the corner of her room sheepishly. Ashapurna devi yelled at him furiously as angry tears dripped down her cheeks, "I have only stayed in this house because of her and education. I have seen it, she is going to be the beacon of light, not only for girls but also for the upcoming generation in entire Kolkata!"Subarnalata was stunned at her mother's roaring voice and the unvarying amount of confidence it resonated ,"You on the other hand want her to get married to some ambitionless and characterless son of some top lawyer, just because it's good for your deal. You are a complete shame for a father. You don't care about her studies at all, but I would ensure that she stands on her feet monetarily. I would stand with her rock solid against you and the entire society if required– "

"Try to understand, nobody wants such an educated wife, they just want a wife."

"No, they just want a doormat who can dance upon their whims and fancies. Do not even DARE to think about that!"

This was like a final call to the entire universe, and no one would dare to intervene in her mother's way. Not even God.

The mouse and Subarnalata scampered back to their comfort zones with stunned silences, "*Katyani* - "Subranalata murmured in her sleep.

The goddess who was known to untap into the unseen and seek beyond the future which would behold the spiritual abundance of the universe. Ashapurna devi had seen the bright future her daughter would behold. The future, that would not only be setting an example to society but had the power to break the generational curses that tied women to the harmful shackles of society.

Subarnalata had not completed her PHD, but her research papers had become the most sought-after study materials of many international students in top universities across the world. Subranalata was still the same and the only change that occurred in her was that her beautiful long locks had been colored brown.Her eyes were bedecked with chocolate colored rim glasses, with Taaru Da's photo between her books. Taaru da on the other hand had kept the dried rajanigandha flowers as his fond distant memory.

she
must be
very
backward
she is so
confident

Shashanya

It is said that during the office time, the temperature in Kolkata can soar to a 65 degree celsius during the summer seasons and so did Shashanyas's temper. Already known for her raging temper and velvety dark skinned she was often referred as tornado.

Shashanya was waiting for her golden chariot and the handsome charioteer which was the NK-101 bus and its pot-bellied bus conductor. The only commute which led straight to her office instead of multiple fickle rides she had to take, which would only lead to a severe spondylitis. After her golden chariot had arrived, Shashanya just rode upon her chariot and plugged her earphone because it would take an eternity to reach to her destination and music was not only soulful to the ears but sometimes, she would just switch on to old Shammi Kapoor songs. They would provide as a good background score to the already comical situation and provided her emotional relief.

As her destination had arrived, she heaved a big sigh of relief and proceeded to battle the long day ahead. Her Sindhi boss was a miser, he would often overwork them and not provide them with a generous bonus amount despite making heaps of profits. Keswani had not only decided their pile up their already overloaded schedule, but it had actually become his ritualistic process to end up at least in a singular conversation which required provocation from his end and a verbal disagreement from hers. This kind of dislikement only stemmed because *Shanshanya* was different. Not only in her physical appearances but also in her personality. She was extremely headstrong and her strong- willed personality worsened the situation for Keswani who never liked being reminded of anything that goes against the tide. This normally meant that woman who do not succumb to the normal standards of society have to go through varied obstacles in life including unwanted and hurtful opinion of others. Shashanya entered her office floor with a big fake smile, the receptionist immediately started giggling. She constantly heard rumors of the infamous fights between Keswani and Shashanya.

"You are late," Keswani exclaimed with a cup of coffee in his hand and a sachet of coffee gold

"So much of a Sindhi," Shashanya thought to herself as she looked at him nonchalantly and said, "I have arrived on time."

"Its10: 10 AM and the office timings are from 10:00 AM," Keswani said crookedly.

"No one has arrived yet." Saying this she glided smoothly towards her desk restarting the office desktop while rearranging her office files expecting a pile of work to engage her for the rest of the day.

Shashanya worked as Financial Analyst and was working with Keswani only for the Job profile as it helped her enhance her finance knowledge. She was also slowly preparing for entrance examinations for big corporate giants as she wanted much more for herself than the job career. She wanted to be a shining star for her family, make her parents proud and make a difference in the society even if it was minimalistic.

For the past few weeks Keswani had been conducting interviews, it seemed like a government bank where all sorts of people came with various problems. The interview often served as a comical delight to the already stale days. Keswani was expanding his office and he required some cheap labour (where college graduates or MBA from mushroom universities would settle down for any PayScale) and he had not found a single scapegoat yet. "Leave alone a few of them," Keswani just mumbled something unintelligent and disappeared into his big lavish office while Shashanya was already focused on her work schedule for the day which was going to be long and tiresome and with limited food breaks which often increased her crankiness.

As the interview sessions consumed Keswani and his moodiness. Shashanya saw this as an opportunity to research for better jobs and apply for those well-defined positions during her mini breaks. After a day's long and backbreaking work with minimal breaks, she decided to leave for the day. At that exact moment with a devilish smile plastered on his face, Keswani appeared smirking with joy and with a heap of piles almost covering his neck from the waist. It appears, the devil had readied his plans and it was her bad astrological timings that could not defer the situation. He delayed her purposefully for one hour. In the background Shashanya could hear his late-night drink plans with his "guy friends", while she sat at her desk sorting the issues in file one by one. As she finished almost eighty percent of the work, she approached him with an exhausted face and all he could say, "Only 80 percent done?" Shashanya rolled her eyes. She was ready to leave for the day when she noticed that he was browsing semi clad pictures of some models to which Shashanya could only roll her eyes. She moved towards her golden chariot and decided it was time for her to move onto a bigger opportunity. Something which provided her mental stability too apart from the financial one.

As she reached home, exhausted, and ravenous, she was blessed that she was working in her hometown and her mother had already switched the geyser and prepared a warm meal which provided her the ultimate soul satisfaction. However, she knew she could not depend upon this arrangement for long and wanted to relieve her ageing mother from same. Moreover, her mother had been pestering her for the marriage arrangement which was very comical situation for her as most of them were looking for customized options as if some pre – ordering of mobile phones and not looking for long term commitments. ***Shashanya*** never understood how her dark skin, or someone's waistline was inversely proportional to the life term long commitment made in this society as she had faced some of the most severe comments related to her skin color. Some even going to the extent of calling her adopted from a poor slum, and it was quite a triggering moment for her as she was also very much fatigued with the usual fights going around in the house regarding her marriage. Her mother's frustration trickled in terms of routine fights with her father and mother.

Shashanya was desperately trying to look for a better career opportunity with a good monetary offer to provide some stability and help pacify her mom. She had thought that her big moves in career would help her to see her daughter in different light and understand that she was way more than the stereotypical conceptualized tamed version of the society. However, "***Beauty is skin deep***" is quite superficial statements which sounded pleasant to the ears but was not practiced around society; Shashanyas mother had practiced all religious rituals and ensured that she literally immolated herself in all the necessary beauty packs also known as uptans in Indian culture which promised to turn a black swan into a white one according to the whitewashed illogical advertisements. Anyway, after all the comical circus playing around the house and in her office, Shashanya often spent her time in Ramakrishna mission where one of the priorities for entry was confiscation of the mobile phones which was extremely soul satisfying and made her oblivious to the outside world. It also introduced her to the world of spiritual books especially on the life lessons of Swami Vivekananda, and advice in life by other Swamiji which helped to soothe her pain and elevate her on spirituality.

As she entered her office the following day, thinking of another battle ahead, she discovered a group of office colleagues who had been gathering around the notice board which had the list of top three winners of ***employee of the month***. However, her name was left out from the list despite of her working hard and providing quality deliverables to the company. Shashanya was beyond appalled and only focused on her upcoming project "*To find better job with Sindhi's wifi*"

She started her days work as Keswani came beaming with joy hoping to find her sullen face elongated. However, to his dismay he found her immune to his foolish tactics and went on mumbling something unintelligent. He went into full operational swing to pot another catastrophe for Shashanya. That very day, Keswani had found an immature and irrational way to find someone to reduce his workload to, at very less pay. It was like hitting two birds with one stone as this was also a method of irritating Shashanya as the girl he chose was not competent enough for the job profile and was very lazy. She was one of the most well-dressed people she had ever met, and it very much was evident that her apt style required much effort. Her innumerable visits to the break area were quite irritating as it was Shashanyas duty to guide her and train her which was very difficult for her to manage along with the work, and this had reduced her time for applying online to varied jobs.

Shashanya was getting tired each day and her health had started deteriorating. It was showing on her face like dark circles, rough skin, droopy eyes etc. She started to think that she would like to resign, restore her health, and spend time on her job application. Coming back home had also become a punishment as her mother was not happy with the delayed timings. She wanted her to spend time on an online matrimonial site daily, for at least one or two hours after work which was not time consuming but also, she was doing the task with a lot of negative vibes which would not lead to any positive fruition. On top of all that, her mother had arranged a dinner meeting with one of the matrimonial prospects next month. So, her daily routine required her to bedeck herself with all the unnecessary beauty packs and eating healthy food at the right time which the only thing keeping her going. Office had become nightmarish for her as she was noticing Keswani's growing fondness towards the new accomplice was only fatal to the company due to the incompetency the girl brought. Her faith was slowly decreasing in her weak astrological placements in the chart. One weekend, she decided to revisit the Ramakrishna Mission and restore her faith in humanity and peace.

Suddenly, a red covered hard bound book caught her attention. It was a brief history of the story on the various incarnations of goddess Kali, out of which "Shashankali" brought a smile upon her face. It emphasized upon the Kalis infamous avatar which was Shashankali who was known for notorious and infuriating temper which would lead to the mass destruction along with the devil slaying. Her skin color resembled the dark night without the stars and moon in the sky. Her long lustrous hair were like the silk satin river stream merging into the ocean. Her beautiful facial features were scarred by the several wars she had waged with many demons and her hand was bejeweled with human skull embellishments. Her chest had been stained with bloodspots dripping from the tongue and at that very moment Shashanya imagined herself in the same image only to be charging towards the battlefield with a bowl filled with blood and a face representing a mixture of anguish and hatred for the entire wrong doings of the mankind. Shashanya was against the entire superficial establishment that mankind had created which had led to the crippling mindset of society leading to weaker personality being bred in the society. Shashanya was tired of violence against women especially the daily taunts and the illogical established standards which required every woman to fit in without their permission and this had made several oppressed women bitter and unhappy.

Shashanya had decided she needs to take not only small steps to do needful but also make a drastic measure in her own personal life which would deter people to take others for granted. One of the major steps she thought was accepting her insecurities and teaching young women across the world on how to accept their raw version. Maybe also admire the beauty standards that women have created for themselves which has no self-harm. This started with an introspection within herself. She had started to write blogs on paid platforms and began motivating other teenagers with positive thoughts and self-acceptance blogs. In office she ensured that she made her huge step by bringing her opinions on table and ensuring that Keswani is strictly brought to the right track. She started by strictly following the office timings, pinpointing when someone else in office did not shoulder the exact responsibility and indirectly referred that elevating another employee without achievement would be a huge impartiality and resulting in good staff leaving the firm. She had seen the horror on Keswani's face which was no less than the female ghosts in South Korean movies as she had emphasized on each syllable and ensured that her words carried reassurance and assertiveness.

Daily, she ensured that she followed a strict health routine and not unnecessary beauty regime that required her to look like a comical version of the ghost portrayed in the Ramsay horror movies. Meditation and yoga were routinely processed for her mental health. She decided to make herself most important and that's what she would follow.

As women, we should realize that we need to channelize the inner power in a constructive manner and not let society or the shortcomings in our life dim our light. Most importantly like Shashankali, we must accept our flaws like smearing ashes on our body and clothe it with confidence. We need to accept the way we are than rather have society tell us about the way we live or the pre standard definition of beauty. We need to worship the goddess within ourselves.

However, as Shashanya saw the goddesses' picture on her calendar before she was retiring to bed, somehow the skull on the goddess's wrist reminded her of the Keswani's growing bald head due to stress caused by her which finally got her into fits of laughter.

BANK
2
she is getting promotion because of her good looks
all customers are surrounding her because of her good looks

Manasa

The ancient Greek temple that was situated near the sea almost seemed like a mirage. With its whitewashed stone wall and the beautiful fountain which seemed so alluring. Each drop of water originating out of it seemed like a crystallized form of water shining like diamonds against the harsh sunrays that too seemed envious of the calm beauty brought on by the temple of Athena against the seashore. Athena the goddess of justice and wisdom was one of the most respected gods as her blessing could bring upon clarity and truthfulness which was the goal of every individual. She was one of those goddesses whose teachings of wisdom had illuminated and improved many lives. Never had anyone heard of any injustice or betrayal of some sort, however all would be changed within a few weeks and the great temple would now be renowned for a tragic story till the end of time.

Medusa was lying on her seashell like bed when her mother Ceta entered the room to wake her daughter up for the customary ritual to be performed before becoming the high priestess for Goddess Athena. For a Minute Ceta, found herself astonished at the picturesque beauty of her daughter lying on bed, Medusa's lair seemed like satin silk that glistened like brown pearls, her white porcelain skin would even put the creator to shame and those fine beautiful eyes even when closed seemed like a delicate lotus bud and the lashes were curly enough to give the exact definition it required.

Ceta was not only proud of her daughter's beauty but also the purity & wisdom with which Medusa carried on in her life. Had they known of the catastrophe that lay Infront of them, they would have never asked Medusa to perform the ceremony at Athena's temple. Medusa walked into the temple, her body bedecked with a white cloth that had succeeded in cloaking her beautiful body but could not conceal the perfect body shape and grace with which it moved. It seemed like an angel had suddenly landed on the seashore. Every person in the temple had been mesmerized by her beauty and the entire thing seemed like a honey trap to attract more visitors and a ploy to become the most prayed goddess.

One day Medusa went to acquire sea water to perform final ritualistic offering that would officially make her the high priestess of the Athena temple. This was making her nervous and very happy at the same time, she thought of washing her face with the sea water to soothe her nerves. As she kept the pitcher near the sand and removed her slippers, she began washing her face with warm salty water which felt different, she started enjoying herself so much that she did not notice that her cloak was completely drenched and was clinging on to her wet body like dew drops on a morning leaf. As her cloak had fallen from the head gear, her long lustrous brown hair was glistening against the sun like a curtain of smooth satin, the glitter against the sea waves had sent an uncontrollable urge to Poseidon- the god of sea to emerge out of the water and intertwine with Medusa. As he arose out of the water body, Poseidon was intoxicated by love seeing the childlike innocence on Medusa's face and in his sudden hypnosis, he carried Medusa forcibly into the temple. While the entire time Medusa was screaming and writhing in pain due to his firm grip against her hips which caused her immense pain, as she was fighting to loosen his grip, several pillars with ritual offerings to Athena had been knocked over the white floor leaving a stain that could now never be removed due to shame.

Poseidon had torn each fragment of cloth on her body which has softened due to wetness of the sea water. He kissed every part of her, Medusa felt as she was being bitten by several snake tongues and her scream was now silenced. Poseidon had entered her forcibly leaving her writhing in pain as her pelvic portion of the body has been thrusted with impure intentions and nothing in the world could restore that. Poseidon had not stopped for several hours and seemed that his thirst was could not be quenched easily. Finally, when he was tired of his own devilish urges, he planted a kiss on Medusas' left cheek who was now subconsciously lying on the floor and had given up on mercy calling of the goddess Athena- While departing he said, "I would be known as the only man in your life till eternity "with these words it seemed like a curse had been laid upon her. That very evening when Medusa could barely stand upon her two frail feet. She fell on Athena's feet asking for justice and mercy while sobbing, Athena finally appeared with a rage like appearance and cursed Medusa for the impurity brought upon by her in the temple, she accused Medusa of bringing lust, greed, vanity into people instead of guiding them to wisdom and light. At that moment, Medusa had been too shocked and was trembling in fear when she noticed that her satin silk hair had been turned into several long venomous snakes that were now making hissing sounds. Her beautiful dazzling eyes had turned into frightful green venomous buttons and anyone staring into them would turn into stone. The temple which was once known for its wisdom, beauty and peace had now turned into a barren cursed land while Poseidon continued to reign as the sea god.

Manasa was now staring at the blank ceiling and almost had gone into a trance. The story had completely dazed her out, she was not aware about which part of the story was more annoying. Was it the fact that gods had committed heinous crime? Athena being a woman had betrayed her fellow community or that Medusa's entire life had immersed into ruins, and it would require a huge karmic intervention from the supreme gods to restore faith in humanity or kindness itself. **Manasa** had been lying on her bed researching about Greek god mythology for her upcoming book – **"Mithras – Myths or Legends"** and to be fair enough most of the content would be dense or controversial given the varied crooked instances of the Greek gods. She heaved a deep sigh which made her hamster look at her curiously. He was desperately waiting for **Manasa** to get up from the bed, stretch along and feed him his evenings snacks. **Manasa** stretched along her bed and sprang up in determination to complete her unfulfilled tasks of the day with full vigor. **Manasa** had just completed her MBA from an esteemed college of Kolkata with her major in Finance and was placed in one of the topmost banks of India as senior relationship manager handling the portfolio of most of the H1NI clients of the city. During her grace period which lasted one month, **Manasa** was focused on completing the book that she had started upon and wanted to keep her creative options open. She was also required a channeling to dissipate her negative energy into a very positive and creative one. The banking sector in her city was quite hectic and demanding. It would consume most of her time. Given the fact she was at the top of her game with her high marks and rankings, she knew she would secure the topmost placement with a good package. Manasa was a keen observer and one of her greatest conclusions was that her city was filled with people who would provide financial advice without even any experience. Leave alone qualification. One of the greatest self-proclaimed financial advisors were the senior citizens who used to come daily in Bhannu'da shop and started advising him on how to procure finances and more importantly how to invest so that his tea stall can become more of a coffee day outlet. However, Bhaanu da would very subtly ignore all the signs as his prime concern everyday would be to weasel out of the two overweight female karmic connections he had in his life (his mother and wife). Having an escapade to an almost alternate reality. Bhaanu da's tea stall was the ultimate sensational destination for any prime visitor, right from the debate at what speed would the storm hit the coast to which milk pouch is better in terms of nutritional elements. The human behavior at its most raw nature was best left to be studied here according to Manasa, especially during the winter months where coffee or jaggery tea were preferred and neither was a specialty in Bhaanu da's stall This emptiness was always filled with Manasa's loyalty which could not be derived out of monetary satisfaction. The unspoken bond between Manasa and Bhaanu da was exquisite and even silence had a deeper meaning between them just like a prodigy and the child.

Manasa's hiatus had fizzled out like most of the cricket tournaments, where so much was happening it was impossible to keep a track and Manasa found herself juggling between several activities. She considered herself like one of those Turkish Ice-creams servers, it was quite tough to determine if it was a trick or an entertainment activity. Manasa's new boss was a Sindhi who preselected employees not based on their ability but whether they could be the ultimate milk ticket which could not only increase his wealth but also make him eligible for the ultimate Sindhi bachelor in the annual Sindhi family gatherings due to his big pocket size, never minding the pea sized brain he owned.

Every day the branch meeting seemed like a comical circus display as most of it was unintelligent conversations and each of the employees were reduced to money making objects. But when it came to Manasa, the Sindhi boss had given it a pass, as he always saw her as an intelligent eye candy who would attract many customers due to looks and pleasant personality and was willing to give it a try to this new glittering stone rather than use his harsh hire and fire policy. Manasa had become really exhausted with the toxic environment created everyday due to her boss's hostility and it was slowly clogging her creativity outlet. The branch meetings revolved around creating fools out of the customers with their polished English vocabulary and manipulating them irrespective of their age, strata of society or gender. The tricksome methods were slowly modifying into unethical money procuring ones which had turned the entire branch into a hostile competitive environment. Job procurement was no longer a source of satisfaction amidst employees. Most of the corporeal jobs had made employees a walking corpse which had stagnated their learning and enhanced the intellectual capacity.

Manasa was amidst a cold war with her Sindhi boss as she had not been able to procure a massive amount of funds. One fine day, the simmering anger between the two had to be vented out and this time the great episode of Mr Lalwani would act as catalyst, Mr Lalwani who a 65-year-old man was, widowed with two children away from their homeland. He wanted to invest in a safe and stable mutual fund and had no intention of diverting away from the plan due to his lack of extensive knowledge in the subject and void in trust with current day bankers. Mr Lalwani had somehow trusted upon Manasa based upon his instinct and her good vibes amidst the dirty environment. Manasa had become fond of her visits to Mr Lalwani as it was a natural escapade into a homely environment away from the toxicity of the banking world and coming into a warm cozy environment. Teaching about the basic concepts of investing to a stranger seemed like an unusual teacher- student relationship. However much it seemed like Mr Lalwani was quite impressed with her conceptuality and decided to take baby steps in investment but promised quite a lump sum amount in the future.

Manasa was content with her achievement. She had earned a loyal educated customer but also knew that this would appear like a miniscule achievement to Mr Keswani (he who must not be named - the Sindhi Boss) and as she was busy devouring the peanuts the local channawala was selling. She started envisioning herself in the channawala's costume and Keswani as the bus - conductor both belonging to the same strata of society yet with varied perspectives. The punch lines and exotic accent that emanated out of the bus conductor was from his paunchiness and his main objective was to extract money out of the passengers sometimes which were standard and sometimes non -

standard rates. The channawala on the other hand was very passionate about his job even though he earned peanuts along with roasting it. He had the serenity on his face that most of the millionaires were lacking even when they had everything. Sighing heavily, Manasa started envisioning how her life would be if she had taken a risk in stepping down from the corporate job and focusing full time on her writing. The more she thought, the darker and gloom she become. As one of the tiers of the bus smoothly dipped itself into the murky potholes, her reflection had shattered her soul. Her weary eyes and pale dull skin were a reflection to her tired soul and a step away from mental exhaustion. Disappointed, she entered the office unaware of the calamity that was lying in front of her. It seems all her banking colleagues including her infamous boss was waiting to pounce upon her to extract the good news of a heavy investment, but the already exhausted Manasa was weary of any choiceable words and had just blatantly told them that the movement was delayed and would be inaugurated with a small but stable investment for the moment. Keswani was simmering with anger and his whole face had turned into a red ugly baboon. However, he controlled his anger and decided to add one of his favorite male bootlickers for her help to turnaround the situation. Manasa was in no mood of banter and quietly agreed to this, knowing, she would have an upper hand on this. On the day of signing of the mutual fund papers, Rahul (boot licker) agreed to take the papers for the signing, as he had a potential client nearby to Lalwani's location. Since Manasa had personally seen to the documents of the paper, she trusted him for once, and agreed. After few days, when Manasa thought the storm had quietened she returned to her traditional ways of locating potential lead, phone directory of the bank which included all the customer details. However, the process seemed tad bit hectic as she felt that the entire process was like that of the late 90's where every trunk call had to go multiple callers, this seemed same as the phone call had to go through various phase like the electricity nodes. First, the call would be picked up generally by a child or servant, either of both would consume more time than the advertisements between two songs in the radio channels which seemed like eternity. If they were able to decipher the ultimate word in the Chinese whisper challenge, the phone would reach the destination which was the actual caller and after reaching the destination, just like we find yellow banners which says bad road ahead, 80 percent of the callers termed it as bad timing and it turned out as a bad failure cut. Manasa started thinking of innovative ways of locating potential lead when a sudden call had interrupted her trail of thought and it was Mr Lalwani and this time she was exhilarated but after a few minutes her entire body had gone cold.

"Manasa!" he almost screamed at the top of his lungs, "I trusted you and ended up being cheated!"

"I don't understand Manasa!" He exclaimed and started stuttering. Manasa was unable to comprehend the reason of this sudden fuming anger.

"Manasa – after our verbal conversation, your colleague Rahul made me sign the work papers and I did it knowing you had sorted the papers. However, after a few days, a huge sum was deducted from my account balance and something which was not negotiated or discussed. I decided to visit another bank branch across the city and found out that it was not a mutual fund papers but insurance workpapers for which I had signed and Rahul had made me return my cheque book saying it was best to give money through UPI ID account number and I did the same, but I'm unable to fathom, how did a large sum get deducted and how did I end up signing Insurance workpapers?!"

Unable to locate the correct words, Manasa started fumbling Lalwani who was enraged understood her silence and found a comfort knowing it was not her involvement in devious ploy that led to this sudden incident. He cut the phone saying goodbye, but Manasa remained on the phone. She was still shocked and unable to speak. Out of the corner of her eye she saw Mr Keswani and the boot licker boys laughing within the conference rooms and giggling away to glory without even a hint of repentance on their faces. Manasa sighed sadly and started to walk towards Bhaanu da's tea stall. He noticed that Manasa was in her unusual mood, it took some time for her to process each word, as she was gulping down huge chunks of shame. Bhaanu da took some time to curate the perfect tea recipe for her and added a pinch of turmeric instead of the usual ginger or cardamom. Every ingredient had its specialty and turmeric was placed on an altar in every Indian heart. It had the potential to lighten up the mood. The aroma of the turmeric and its taste blended into her soul and immediately provided her the instant satisfaction she required, after drinking it she seemed tosettled down. Bhaanu da asked her candidly, "What happened ma?", to which Manasa again returned to a world of gloominess. Bhaanu da had explained her that often the bootlickers and Keswani used to frequent the tea stall. They would discuss, laugh, and mimic most of the clients and used to make fun of them, she even discovered that they had kept a code name for her, and it did not take Bhaanu da long to decipher it which was "candy bar" This saddened Manasa rather than making her angry. She grew despondent at the plight of the society. Bhaanu da told her how often they used to discuss boys' night out plans always leaving Manasa out. All these discussions were taken lightly by Bhaanu da until one day he found out that they were plotting against Mr Lalwani. They discussed how they would exchange the work papers and Keswani would speak to his boss regarding the change of plan in investment. In any case of any shoddiness, they would burden her with blame.

The melancholic evening slowly gave way to early night. She realized that she had become incredibly late for her home ride and had also missed her scheduled bus trip, so she decided rush at this hour. Upon entering the office, she saw a group of boys in a huddle having the same filthy expressions she had vividly imagined. She hurriedly grabbed her bag and rushed towards the bus stop as she was waiting for her ride, she realized that the boys never asked whether she would be able to reach home safely which was basic courtesy. chivalry should be deleted from the dictionary itself.

As she was waiting for her ride and chewing her lower lip nervously because of the late timing, she finally saw a ray of hope with a bus approaching towards her route and heaved a big sigh of relief.

However, as she was climbing the stairs of the bus, she noticed that the bus driver was slightly drunk, and his devilish smile was scarier than his red swollen eyes. She slowly tiptoed into the bus and chose the second seat in case she had to rush out.

She saw the bus driver watching her every move stealthily and slowly which was making her feel extremely uncomfortable and her face was slowly whitewashed with fear. She carefully slid her hand inside the bag to locate if anything familiar could remotely save her life if necessary. However, she realized she even didn't carry the deodorant which could act like pepper spray. The bus was moving in the right direction, and she was just counting on the moments when she could arrive to her destination safely and then she just saw a flicker of light flashing on her face which is because the bus conductor was now flashing the torch on her face and smirking all the way through while asking for the fare. She kept her mind composed and tried to avoid showing dismay on her face which could lead to something dangerous.

After he took the fare from her, she felt as if the bus driver was winking at him as if to give a green signal to act upon something, and she felt he was drawing closer to her. She just yanked the collection purse out of his arm and punched his gut, the bus driver came to a halt. She took that chance and just waited for bus to become steady and ran for her life. She turned around just in time to capture the bus number in case she had to follow up and go to police.

Before reaching home, she decided to smoothen out her attire and remove all the collected dust so as not to worry to her mother. She straightaway headed towards the washroom to freshen up and have dinner and rest. After she completed her activities for the day she went to rest and started thinking of the *Chapter: Medusa* and her reaction to how the divine lady was reprimanded without any fault of hers. She decided the very moment at how she had swinged a full blow on the conductor's face; she had decided to give a very strong message to her male office colleagues who had been bullying her throughout the time.

The very next day Manasa decided to go to the HR portal and lodge an official complaint on how she felt outcasted and belittled by her male colleagues. She wanted to feel secure and stable in the job. The very same day the HR had taken the matter very seriously and had decided to take the issue in their hands. As she entered the bank the very next day, she decided to call a new day and start with a fresh new breath.

As she swung open the door, she saw the face of her new boss. Beaming with joy upon seeing her potential candidate, she immediately felt like Medusa, only renewed much stronger and ready to take upon a new challenge with open arms and positivity.

People criticize a lot in this beauty industry
Future is bright in this beauty blogging industry

Soundarya

The Dice has spoken for itself, she is ours now and immediately thereafter a devilish laughter broke out in the courtroom, it seemed that the earth stood still and all the gods had frozen to the horrific event that would take place eventually in the due course of time. The five Pandavas were bowing down their head in shame. Shakuni's evil plan and smile was spreading like the plague in the courtroom, what astonished the gods above was that the court was filled with warriors known across lands for their bravery and physical strength. However, if there had been an integrity test somewhere on all these so-called brave men, they would have failed terribly and wouldn't even be able to be called men. As Paanchali was being dragged to the court and her pain filled voice pierced through the room like God himself was yelping in pain. Dushashan imposed his muscular strength on Paanchali as he grabbed her hair and dragged through the court room. Her hair had been disheveled and her cloth that had been draping her beautiful, yet muscular figure was now being displaced. Glimpses of her skin were enticing the men in the courtroom. Arjuna was bowing his head in shame and droplets of tears which were as precious as jewels were trickling down his cheeks. He secretly vowed to seek revenge for the despair brought upon his family and himself, he kept staring at the strands of hair fallen across the courtroom, he always considered his gandeeva to be the greatest weapon in the universe but now it looked inferior compared to the fierceness, yet despair filled eyes of Paanchali. He vowed in that very moment that not only would he seek revenge, but he would ensure that a cosmic event would take birth which would stay in the universe and forbid many in the future to think or treat a woman poorly. He remembered his truest friend Krishna in the moment of despair and thus gave birth to the idea of the greatest war that ever occurred.

Soundarya was reading the latest mythological book that was gifted to her, it was by the bestseller author whose writings were based on Indian Mythology, the books were not only pearls of wisdom but were embedded with his opinions that regulated with the masses and established the fact that righteousness should always win in the end and should also be implemented in our day to day lives. Soundarya's eyes were droopy, and she was almost drowsing in sleep. She was vividly imagining in her sleep that she was standing in the centre on the same spot where Paanchali was lying with her face down and was still crying with her face on the ground. While Soundarya bent down to pull Paanchali towards her and console her, she heard an eruption of sudden laughter that echoed throughout the courtroom like mockery. She was pulling Paanchali towards her when she saw familiar faces like her society aunties who gossiped about her, relatives who secretly wished her bad and her cousins who pretended to be good but were pointing and laughing at her. Their laughter had the tone of deep mockery and subtle hints of jealousy, and she suddenly saw these same people picking up stones and throwing at her distinctively.

Soundarya got up immediately and found herself completely covered with beads of sweat which had enveloped her completely from head to toe. Her knees were trembling with fear while she put her head over her them and started to take in deep breaths to calm herself down. She went downstairs towards the kitchen to compose herself with herbal tea or lukewarm milk with cardamom. However, as she saw there was minimal milk left in the pan, she decided to offer that portion to the cat named Vasco which could give her midnight company while she sipped onto her herbal tea to calm her nerves. She saw a sudden flicker of light in the opposite building, where her sly neighbor and her mother lived and were officially the lame version of Byomkesh Bakshi. Their primary objectives were to draw two columns and compare her daughter to others, Soundarya was the prime competitor as apparently, she was born with flawless milky white skin which seemed like a glistening crystal glassware. Some even called her snow white of the Bengal land. Her friends during her young age concocted a rhyme like "*Mirror Mirror on the wall, Soundarya is the milkmaid of Bengal*". Her white complexion was a subject of envy for every mother in her locality whose prime rivalry had escalated to such a high level where they had subjected their daughter to unnecessary beauty regime just to compete with Soundarya.

Soundarya heaved a sigh of relief as she remembered those bountiful days when she had lot of friends with whom she spent many memorable and fun filled days but eventually her group had been reduced to one or two genuine friends including Vasco her cat. After she composed herself, she realized it was midnight and Vasco had eaten all the mice in her house, so there was no chance of any god mother appearing in front of her to grant all her wishes. She slowly tiptoed towards her room sent the lizard back to its haven which was the famous Mona Lisa painting. Somehow the Mona Lisa painting enchanted and mesmerized her, she felt it had a hypnotic draw towards it. She seldom found herself pondering over the fact whether it was Mary Magdalene indeed who had captivated Da Vinci's thoughts, or the story had another mysterious character entirely.

She just left for her room and fell asleep immediately as she fell onto the bed.

To put an emphasis on Soundarya, she was not only beautiful, but she had graduated as an MBA in Finance and had been working in the Finance Industry for the past five years. She was doing quite well in her job as a senior financial analyst in an esteemed multinational company and was earning quite well. However, she had faced several hiccups during her career as she was known for her beauty more than her meritorious work. This has caused several issues in her career as most of the men were extremely enchanted by her beauty and wanted to have close work discussion with her. However, their prime objective was to know is she was readily available. Soundarya lay farfetched from the idea of romance or anything close to it as she wanted bloom around authentic relationships which made her feel content and secure. Her mother always taught her that one should learn to differentiate between need and want based connection. One should learn to thrive on the latter as it not only provided contentment but also helped us get rid of bad karma.

Soundarya was really thriving to be a top financial analyst at her job however she found it difficult with her neat and clean nature and only sheer hard work. She was aiming to get selected at the topmost company which could help her attain her desired position and job profile. She secretly also wanted to live independently outside the city and discover her true potential. Soundarya had quite a bucket list of things that she wanted to achieve and discover her inner true feminine power. She quickly had bonded well with her brooding rough edged financial management books which could provide her with the emotional and monetary contentment.

The next weekend morning Soundarya got up a bit late wishing it would soak away all the tiredness and would rejuvenate her from the entire week's frustration. She had also enrolled herself in swimming classes which helped her dissipate all the negative energy and maintain her competitiveness. She was about to head out of the house after gobbling her entire breakfast meal in one bite but for the first time she laid her eyes upon her, and little did she know that the saree clad lady standing in front of her would not only have a profound effect on her life but a remarkable change in her thought process.

Sundari was one of those ethereal beauties who so naturally gifted that even when she sobbed, her face would glow up making her look like a fallen angel and she would end up making the opposite person look like a devastated fool. Sundari was of the same age as Soundarya, and she had been married at an early age which she never regretted as she was gifted with a precious husband. However, her dream to study further remained unfulfilled. Sundari had seen her parents been murdered and she would have wanted to seek revenge on her murderers which were her own uncle and aunty. However, her weak demeanor, delicate nature, and unknowingness about the harsh realities of the world made her resort only to sobbing profoundly. Soundarya's mother was very close to Sundari's mother, and she knew momentarily that she had to rush to her mother's friend and to seek refuge in her house and her arms. Sundari started giving a helping hand to Lata di, Soundarya's mother in the household as she wanted to feel the maternal love and security. Soundarya also started pouring her sisterly love towards Sundari and started showing small tokens of gestures like gifting her new dresses to getting her confectionery.

One day as Soundarya was returning from her daily work almost exhausted from the commuting and wanted to collapse right into the arms of her bed which was almost calling her for embracement. She entered her room and was welcomed with the aroma of jasmine. She saw a remarkable improvement in the layout of the room and her bed was laid out with fresh bed sheets which also seemed scented. She saw the old haggard yellow bulbs being replaced with lotus shaped crystal emanating soft pink lights. She first decided to pinch herself as she thought it was a product of her drowsiness and her imaginations has started to leak out of her subconscious. She sat down on the sofa and was still processing the mild pleasant transformation, when she saw a lady entering the room and for a moment that lady resembled like a Apasara whose hair was tied into a bun and embellished with a garland of flower. A saffron cloth draped around her body in a one shoulder format from an ancient mythological fiction, the scene was blurry and suddenly it seemed that' she snapped out of her hallucination when felt like a sharp pinch on her forearm. She felt a warm liquid falling onto her lap,

"What is the issue? "Soundarya snapped and saw Sundari purposefully putting the warm cup of tea against her forearm to make her snap out of her dream.

"How do you like the room?" Sundari asked blatantly and Soundarya started at her instinctively.

"You did this? Why would you go through so much pain when you already have tons of chores to do?"

"Well..." Sundari said confidently, "You manage to take your time off and gift me things to lift my mood and I can't repay you with small efforts. I requested Lata Ma for the bulbs, fresh bedsheets, and the new vase, she was planning to implement upon her already delayed actions, but I decided to leap upon those as soon as she mentioned. How did you like the décor?"

Soundarya was listening to her intently and was quite amazed by her. She was infatuated by the ethereal beauty she possessed and the also the confidence she was slowly exuberating at this point. A year after the unfortunate incident had taken place, she started fumbling something unintelligent, "Its perfect<" was all she could say in a disinterested voice.

Sundari rushed off towards the kitchen to warm up her food and give her new friend the privacy she required. Soundarya had just gotten out of her shower and after her daily ritual she was famished. She really thought a delicious meal and a good night sleep could rejuvenate herself for the long tiring weekend she was preparing herself for like a warrior. As soon as she walked towards the kitchen, she was surprised to find herself lost to the aroma of the food. The layout of the kitchen seemingly looked different, and her biryani was served on her favourite plate, but the sheets looked different and a new flower vase with fresh scent of the Jasmine flowers was filling the whole house. She immediately knew that Sundari was starting to heal, and this was one of the first evidence she could lay her eyes on. The creativity portrayed by her through interior décor. She was smiling to herself throughout her meal prepared by her mother and the end of the day had been special as she headed off towards her room for a good night sleep.

Soundarya was walking towards a lush green forest while the strong wind was forcing the trees to sway wildly, and the moon seemed quite different. It seemed to be red with slight anger, as Soundarya was going deep into the forest, she noticed that the wind was almost howling in pain. Suddenly she heard a rustling sound near the bushes, and she expected some wild animal to come out of bushes when she heard murmurs in the woods, she started walking towards those voices and saw three figures standing in the dark talking amongst themselves in a hush voice. "They have some equipment's in their hands, they must have come for animal hunting," Soundarya whispered to herself. As she approached them, she saw Sundari lying on the ground, her face distorted and smeared with what seemed to be blood. She seemed to have lost consciousness, as she lay on the ground, the smugness on the faces of the three people was enough for

Soundary to detect the culprit.She rushed towards Sundari to rescue her but a sheath of fine glass appeared to have made a barrier between them and now. The three people were dragging Sundari towards a pit intentionally created to bury her alive, Soundarya kept screaming and banging at the glass door and they kept dragging Sundari and finally flung the body into the pit.

Soundarya woke up hastily and found herself covered in blanket of sweat, she could feel the moistness of her sweat on the bedsheet too. She composed herself and thought that a cup of herbal tea could lighten her up and she headed towards the kitchen. As she tiptoed, her inner protectiveness decided to check on Sundari, she opened the door quietly and saw that Sundari was trembling with fear, and she was speaking in her dreams in a fearful tone. Soundarya quickly went to the hug Sundari and gently lifted Sundari onto her lap and started singing lullaby. She wanted to wake Sundari to gentleness, so the song slowly made Sundari realize she was having a difficult dream and quickly she recovered from it. It did not take much time to understand the nature of nightmare, they slowly tiptoed towards kitchen and Soundarya made Sundari sit on the kitchen table, while preparing tea. Vasco also decided to join the party and started devouring his almond flavored milk, which was a special concoction prepared by Soundarya to calm everyone during the night.

Instead of talking about nightmare they started deviating from the topic and started speaking on random topics from Taaru da's sweaty hands preparing magical tea to Mrs Byomkesh Byokshi who had now been trying to decode their body language as if trying to eavesdrop from their kitchen. Vasco gave a cute yawn seemingly bored with the ladies' conversations and started slurping back its flavor of the night.

It took Vasco's deep purr during its sleep to understand that they had passed two hours in the middle of night just talking about random topics and suddenly both were feeling lighthearted. They decided to retire to bed and finally get a good night sleep. As Soundarya was tucking herself to sleep, she realized that sometimes communication is the key as it makes the heart lighter and then she finally decided to deepen her bond with Sundari, as both required healing from the past. She heaved a big sigh of relief and fell asleep.

Next morning, she woke up a bit late and was literally rushing to office. In a hurry she realized that she had forgotten to wear her vest in the beneath her kurti and no one had bothered to notify her verbally but decided to blatantly stare at her making her feel uncomfortable. Soon it seemed that all the stares were piercing through her back. Later in the washroom she realized that her new bra was fitting her so well attenuating her figure to a large extent making everyone gawk at her uncontrollably. That very afternoon, one of the project managers had kept one hour meeting in the remote corner room of second floor, the conference room did not have any CCTV cameras. She was quite puzzled at the duration and nature of the meeting as the project she had embarked upon was almost at its fag end and it did not require any second authority level review. She has not submitted the finalized projects to the US clients, so she seemed clueless at the nature and duration of meeting. The project manager who was in his late thirties, Mr Sharma often used to check her out openly owing to the power of his designation and authority and this had made her uncomfortable to a large extent. She used to find escapades. Later that afternoon, Soundarya decided to skip lunch and nibble some cafeteria biscuits and lemon tea composing herself just before the meeting. Soundarya slowly tiptoed towards the conference room and waited to plan her seating way before Mr Sharma entered the premises, but she was shell shocked to see him seated before and communicating something important over telephone. He did not even notice Soundarya entering the room and kept on quoting deadlines and numbers.

As Soundarya seated herself in the chair, positioning herself carefully to avoid the wardrobe malfunction. As soon as Mr Sharma got off the phone, he looked at Soundarya heaving a sigh of relief and blatantly stared at her. He asked her about the current situation of the project and about the deadlines when suddenly, he started smudging his eyes. Soundarya started to feel uncomfortable under his gaze and suddenly in between the conversations he broached the topic of lunch with him on a weekend, this really confused her and sent jitters of nervousness in her body. As Soundarya wanted to be fixated on her project, he found some ways to approach the topic of lunch. Finally in despair she said she wanted to focus on the professional aspect and lunch on weekends would only make it unprofessional in nature. This infuriated Mr Sharma who was trying his best to conceal his disdain, but his face had reddened by then and he decided to lean much closer towards her face and ask her to join for lunch. Soundarya's face almost turned red as she was agitated by the threat she received and she knew no way out of the situation, so she composed herself for a minute and was taken aback when he laid his hand on her arms. This angered a lot to which she jerked off from the chair causing it to spin full speed, to this Mr. Sharma got extremely angry and just said,

"The meeting is over." and then he left hastily towards his cubicle. Soundarya was speechless for a moment, it took her sometime to compose herself as she left for home. That day she went to Taaru da's stall and requested him to make a good cup of ginger tea even though he was wrapping up the stall. However, seeing her teary-eyed face, he decided to make his specialty rather than jump into an argument. As she entered her home, she could smell the delicious aroma of dal wafting in the air and it should have lifted her mood. However, she felt the urge to wash herself and soak in some hot water to relieve the stress. She switched on the pink lights and washed herself clean. As she came outside the washroom, she saw Sundari waiting for her near the table with a glass of juice, she looked worried as Soundarya did not greet her and preferred to go straight away to her room.

“Hi – “Soundarya said trying her best to conceal the anguish and pain.

Sundari raised the glass of juice, and Soundarya gulped it down in one go without any hesitation to avoid conversations. She knew Sundari could read her mind and would know something is wrong, but Sundari just gestured her for dinner.

That night, Soundarya felt restless and felt the urge to sleep and drown herself in her subconsciousness, but varied kind of emotions were resurfacing. She woke up early that morning and decided to go for a long walk trying to breathe in fresh air, hoping to dissipate negative energy. As she freshened up and waited to gorge on her breakfast, she noticed Sundari was looking at her intently and her mother was blabbering away something unintelligent. Soundarya left for office to find an HR meeting waiting for her, she knew that Mr Sharma had played his cards. As she approached the meeting, she found out that the HR was awaiting with a small packet in her hand, she just formally introduced herself. The HR cited few unnecessary miniscule events and certain behaviors which were cited on behalf of Mr Sharma and basically it was a termination letter sugar coated in the form of exit process "*If she decides to keep her mouth shut*".

Soundarya did not fight back and wanted to exit the organization too. She has already decided on her next career move, she just was not in a good frame of mind to take the necessary step. She left the organization quickly and sat by the Ganges for a while watching the sunset. As she saw the sun setting towards the west direction, a boatman happened to have been singing "*Ekla cholo re*" written by Rabindranath Tagore. This was often sung by her mother during difficult times. The lyrics of the song filled the air and resonated with her. Generally, she never preferred street food but today she preferred gorging on the peanuts.

As she entered her home, she did not tell her mother about the unfortunate incident occurring in her life and just said that she would be taking off for two days as she had a slight headache and wanted some rest. That very night, Sundari entered her room and this time lifted Soundarya's head and lay on her lap and started humming lullaby to comfort her in sleep, she did not even ask her about the sudden change in the behavior. Soundarya just got up and hugged Sundari.

She recited the entire story and started sobbing uncontrollably.

Sundari comforted her and just asked her one question "What is the name of this shrewd person?" Soundarya just spitted out the name in disgust and kept on sobbing and rested on her shoulders. After a few minutes Soundarya and Sundari both went back to sleep but Soundarya had taken an oath that she would put her level best in forgetting about the situation and move on positively.

Next morning Soundarya got a call from the HR to meet her urgently and she had to reach the premises on a short notice. As she wanted to collect her exit letters soon as possible, she met the HR in a different conference room, and this pacified her to a large extent. The HR seemed tensed and almost pounced upon her as she entered the room,

"Hey Soundarya. Hope you have been fine. I have been meaning to contact you since last evening."

"Hi..." Soundarya fumbled and seemed a bit clueless.

"Soundarya, did you communicate our decision to anyone?"

"Umm, no. Why?" Soundarya fumbled again, seemingly clueless and looking at the HR 's face for answers.

The HR breathed a heavy sigh of relief and relaxed back into the chair

Mr Sharma called back and asked me to pull back the termination workpapers and said to provide you with another chance as you have lot of praises and recognition from the US counterparts.

"But I don't understand...." Soundarya started stammering.

The HR explained that Mr Sharma was called by a senior partner regarding the termination and told to pull back the papers and get hold off the situation.

Soundarya seemed clueless, the HR told her to resume work from next day onwards and walked off towards her next HR meeting.

Soundarya decided to embark upon a boat ride near the Ganges and process what has been happening and this time she made a call to her home landline vide the local telephone booth. She called Sundari and asked her to meet at the Ganges. It had been a while since she has last spoken to Sundari and rather projected her conflict upon her. She wanted to have some light moments with her.

As Sundari came to the spot after much hustle as she was not used to frequenting around the town, so it took her few nudging and pushing with the crowd. Finally reached the spot panting. As she met Soundarya she straightway asked her for water, and almost sat down near the sand area with a thud, Soundarya got up and got her few roasted peanuts and coconut water which almost seemed like elixir as it went down her throat and soothed her parched throat.

As Sundari's panting slowed down, Soundarya briefed her about the incident, and started reciting about the sudden turnover of events and how she seemed clueless about her next step.

"I just want your opinion on what to do next. Should I rejoin the same place or look for another job as I'm not comfortable sharing space with the violator?"

Sundari smiled cleverly and said "Do not worry about that swine. I have dealt with him in my own way."

Soundarya was taken aback, "What....?" she fumbled, "What did you do?"

Sundari recited how she saw one of the senior manager's names in her file and found his address on the business card. She went to that address and recited that very incident to the manager who luckily happened to beMr Sharma's boss. After hearing the whole story, Mr Kundra was very much observant and did not quickly believe Sundari's word, rather he went to have a quick call with the HR.

The HR seemed very nervous to get a call at an odd hour and somehow also blabbered additional details out of nervousness that two employees had been in the similar situation, and she found the resemblance of the situation very uncanny. She herself found Mr Sharma's gaze extremely uncomfortable. Mr Kundra listened to every word intently and after weighing both the incidents he had called upon Mr Sharma to have chat. It seems that Mr Sharma was too nervous to have a talk and admitted the entire mistake. He admitted to his fault and agreed for a written apology to Soundarya and was left off by given a final red warning.

After Sundari finished her story, Soundarya was left speechless and was staring at her face with her jaw almost touching the ground.

"But how did you do know about the incident?"

Sundari just stared into her eyes intently and just spoke calmly "You are not the only one who can assume about the entire incident through dreams. You see I have this gift since childhood, I can send or receive messages through fifth dimensional realm and sometimes I can astral travel through and this time it was easy because I am spiritually connected with you because we are soul sisters. I do not want you to go through the same situation that I have gone through. Though I cannot control life situations, but I can always be your protector and try to salvage the situation."

Soundarya at this point was clueless and speechless and decided that with time she would attain logical answers with the course of time, she just wanted to spend some time with Sundari and munch on the roasted peanuts made with passion and sweaty hands. Soundarya watched the sunset with glory and this time it seemed different. She just missed Vasco at this point, his purring would have painted the complete picture. She vowed that day that she would soon contact her lawyer friends and ensure that at least her house that is legally owned by Sundari can be given back to her.

Somewhere in the parallel universe, Paanchali was smiling as Bheem poured Dushashan's blood over her head; her hair which had been parched for several years was now quenched with revenge. She felt that all the women on this planet who had been wronged at some point had been blessed today.

Tears of contentment were running down Arjuna's dirt-stained cheeks, purifying the skin to reveal the glow he felt from within. All these years of sacrifice had finally been fruitful, he just shot an arrow up in the sky. There were showers of lotus flowers that bedecked Paanchali's hair, and her smile was uncontrollable. Finally, justice had prevailed, and history would remember this day.

What is she doing' witchcraft?
My herbal concoction would be perfect

Mahamaya

The mist was slowly clouding the entire galaxy and suddenly the mortals living on earth were suddenly perplexed as the calendar never predicted an eclipse or equinox or any other event. The Earth and other planets went dark with misery as even the stars refused to shine bright. It seemed that that sorcery was at its best play – Hecates closed her eyes and started murmuring to the universe while her parents Asteria and Perses were looking upon her with proud eyes. She was enacting one of her most powerful performances and playing one of the most pivotal roles in Titanochomy. Zeus looked at her and smiled knowingly that with her help the victory would soon be attained – Hecates slowly channelized her inner power and covered each of the Olympian with a white shield which would protect them from each arrow or any weapon that touched them. The mist had some magical powers which helped the Olympians foresee the next move of the Titans. Hecates was shining to glory, as most of them feared her and considered her some vicious woman whose basic propaganda was to create havoc but today, she seemed to look beautiful with her pale white skin sparkling even in the dim light and her long lustrous hair crowned upon her head seemed like a glittery blanket. The day seemed magical, Zeus smiled more and more as his powers kept increasing, he blessed Hecates within that someday the world would recognize her magical powers as blessings rather than witchcraft or sorcery.

There was a sudden discomfort between her legs, and she could feel a sudden surge of wetness and it suddenly alarmed her to refresh herself before the blood could stain the bedsheet. She quickly leaped up from the bed and rushed to the washroom, she hurriedly grabbed the napkin from the cupboard and went to refresh herself. After she finished her program which now seemed like a ritualistic process every month and now seemed to be a part and parcel of every woman's life. She decided to plunge back into her bed, to check the Hindu calendar, and made a red circle on the date.

"Who knew tik tack or tock, whatever we played during our childhood would play such a pivotal role in a woman's life. I can be a champion any day," she sighed and noticed that her menstruation mostly fell near the new or full moon. This time it fell on Lunar eclipse. Mahamaya's love for reading had no genre limits, somehow her reading for astronomy had also acted as a catalyst for her interest in astrology which were very much interconnected.

As she plonked on her bed waiting for her sleep to reconnect again, she started to think about the preparation and effects of lunar eclipse. It is said that in ancient times the menstrual cycle of a highly spiritual woman related to the moon cycles. The cycle of the new moon was termed as white cycle and the full moon as red cycle. The spiritual woman who bled during the red cycle were often feared in society and this resulted in an oppression- woman movement against the women spiritual leaders by many eminent authoritative people .

So many women, who were gifted, blessed with great manifestation powers but were burnt in the middle of the town cursed, beaten, and termed as sorcerers.

"Pheww! That's pretty heavy stuff," Mahamaya muttered to herself, definitely not a sweet lullaby thought or some candy bubble gum fairy tale.She decided to sleep to some good spiritual flute music

Mahamaya was a highly spiritual woman, and she was working in an esteemed financial organization. She also spent a good amount of time blogging about her thoughts in the form of articles which had a tinge of Satire Comedy. Maya was named after *Mahamaya-goddess Parvati*. Her mother had given birth to Maya on the auspicious day of Durga Astami, however little did her mother know that Mamamaya would shorten her name to appear cool and would not indulge in the performance of the ritualistic process. Mahamaya may not indulge in the ritualistic process but believed in the one God concept-The humanitarian approach. She also believed in the magical process of the universe. According to Mahamaya, the cosmic events occurred by the universe were created by a female goddess, if woman could give life, birthing the entire universe would be a child's play for the goddess. According to Mahamaya, the cosmic events right from the design of the galaxy, solar system, constellation and even the astrological events were like a magical recipe cooked by the great goddess Parvati also known as Annapurna.

Mahamaya was a voracious reader, and her passion started with basic genre like fictional reading. She soon started to gravitate towards other subjects like astronomy, astrology, and other subjects. Her curiosity had no limits, and this resulted in a heap of books being piled up in her library room. This was giving a sore eye to her mother and greed to the *raddiwala (men who made money from selling old newpapers and other items).* Mahamaya was very thrilled to become the member of the Aurobindo Bhavan Library and was submerged into books so much that the old, rugged furniture seemed antique to her. Until one fine day she actually fell down from the chair ignoring the tweaking of the chair which seemed like some meteor passing by in the cosmos and in her dream she was running after a butterfly but only the crash of the meteor seemed soothing to her.She realized later that the old librarian uncle was irritated and now they had to go through the trauma of finding a file amidst a huge pile of books that too hidden by a huge cobweb disturbing the spiders schedule, it would be troublesome for both.

That week Mahamaya was literally limping trying to avoid her mother temper's tantrums, later that evening when she had gone for walk, her old crabby neighbor thought she was duplicating his moves and taunting him, little did he know readers had to go to their share of pain too.

"The curse of the mind," she muttered and believed she could finish the books, on how women were treated during the 1650 and how the puritans claimed any woman seeking and preaching spiritual knowledge related to the universe and their beliefs. Opinions were not only disregarded but they were shamed by society by being termed as witches who were ought to be burnt in the middle of the town. Woman citing examples for other woman who were not to be followed is the same approach of the Salem witch trials. It was very painful to read through the events that followed through which were churned tremendous pain in Mahamaya's stomach making her feel nauseous. The eclipse was anyways having its effect on her.

She decided to retire to bed early not knowing that she would be caught up in a whirlpool of dreams, where the universe would be showing several incidents to guide the light for most of her soul tribe.

Later that night, she saw many future events like the neighbor's cat being rolled over by a water truck with the plate number 6666, the old neighbor who limped almost tripped near the stairs causing a major fracture and the kid near the house corner trying to run away from a pack of dogs as he scratched himself from the mirror of the car while trying to escape from the hound of dogs trying to chase them.

Next morning Mahamaya woke up with a heavy head and asked her mother for a special medicinal concoction to ease her head. Her mother had softened up on her since the unfortunate library event and was pretty much serving her dishes to her preference. Later during the day, she decided to visit the old crabby neighbour and Mrs Roy whose precious cat named "*Chesire*" was treated like their child. Mrs Roy had a lovely mini garden, and she had the most beautiful hibiscus mini plants of blue, white, pink, and of course the traditional red ones which almost matched the wall colour of her house. She did not have a child, so she often nurtured the abandoned and street pets with love and care.

As Mahamaya was approaching towards Roy house, she saw Mrs Roy had just finished watering the plants and was feeding Chesire with utmost tenderness and fondness, Chesire had his own named bowl with Alice in Wonderland prints on it and a baby spoon which was so cute. Chesire had almond shaped hazel eyes which during the night sparkled like green emeralds especially when lights stared at him directly. As Mahamaya stepped on the porch, she was mesmerized by the beauty of the mini garden there was even a small chair for Chesire which had handwoven cushions. The garden had several mini mud castles made for the enjoyment of Chesire. Mahamaya was spell bound by the exclusive creativity displayed by her, she was in the moment, trying to understand on how to approach the situation with sensitivity. As Mrs Roy sensed an outsider's alert, she quickly adjusted her moon reserved for guests. She hardly talked to anyone but was often courteous to all the neighbours.

"Maya!" Mrs Roy exclaimed, "What brings you here? Some exciting news or is there anything you want?

"Nothing.I was just passing by..." Maya blabbered

"I'm just fine! Do you wish to have some sweets? I have made some."

"No Mrs Roy. It's just that I had a premonition about Cheshire, I must forewarn you about the upcoming events. I think you should be careful with him; I do believe he might have an accident if not taken care of properly especially by a 6666 numbered truck."

Mrs Roy seemed dazed, clueless, and shocked to this sudden notification which came out of nowhere without any reference points. She was taken aback.

"I'm sorry! I didn't mean to disturb your peace," and she just ran away as fast as she could.

As she was running she saw her cranky old neighbor and thought of forewarning him too and this time she was about to use choiceable words and modulate her tone. As she approached him, she delivered the same messaged only this time very politely, However, it seemed the astrological placements were wrong that sent Maya into a despair. As the neighbour started to howl, his reaction sent her into despair as she straightaway ran into her mother's arms. Her mother was cooking a fish delicacy with too much cautiousness and started rebuking her. This time Maya started crying and went straightaway to her bed and buried her head into the pillow.

As the evening approached, Maya was listening to a beautiful spiritual hymn to the goddess Parvati when her mother entered the room with a hot cup of herbal tea. She started caressing her daughter's hair and said that she would was preparing special dinner for her, so she was annoyed when she was disrupted suddenly.

"Come on. Forget everything, a warm meal cooked with love can eradicate pain. I even prepared rose sherbet for you, now come one, be a good girl!"

Maya heaved a big sigh of relief and approached her dinner table calmly; she devoured the food as if there was no tomorrow and after she savoured each grain of rice. She gulped it down with her rose sherbet.

She decided to top the feel-good factor with an excellent night's sleep without any astral travel or premonitions. She knew rice in every Bengali's personal cuisine was an excellent choice for a deep sleep and she dozed off while humming the song "*Money, Power and Glory*" She visualized her bank account exploding with a lumpsum money and she was drowning in it. That was one of the best feelings in the world.

Next morning, she decided to walk barefoot on the grass, practice yoga, meditation and do some plucking from personal garden. Mahamaya had her own herb garden, her best friend Neil had known her passion of reading and decided to gift her a book which can cultivate into passion.As she had a barren portion on the back of the yard which could be fertile, till now she had few essential plants like coriander, lemongrass, basil, lemon and also a local plant which was excellent for the crown chakra. Maya plucked a few essential basil leaves, which helped relieving the mental stress and removed the blockage of the throat chakra when put in boiling water. This was her general ritualistic process during the menstruation or low times. As she was inhaling the concocted water, she suddenly was transported to a different realm which was a totally new experience for her. She saw her future self in a spur of the moment surrounded by flash of cameras and a new accomplice who understood the spiritual changes she was undergoing. Additionally, she saw that there was mini crowd in front of Mrs Roy's house and people looked worried and looked skeptically towards her. She just stepped back away from the boiling pot and started breathing heavily. That's when her mother stepped into the kitchen and had a pleasant smile on her face,

"What a nice aromatic smell! The whole kitchen smells like a sweet herb and your face even looks fresh."

Maya looked mortified but she composed herself, while her mother kept blabbering about the culinary items to be prepared this week, as she expected a few of her husbands' colleagues to visit the weekend. Maya started to brace herself trying to suck herself out of the whirlpool.

She decided to indulge in a good book which would calm her mind and let these bizarre thoughts run out of her mind, she chose a typical children's classic book which was also one of her favorite's '*Matilda*'- a book which dealt a super intelligent child with superpowers and how she fit into the world even though her own parents denied her gifted abilities. This book had also culminated into a Hollywood movie which had given inspiration to many children and adults.

As she was reading the book, she felt confused, and tears started rolling down from his eyes. She felt extremely lonely and felt that' she needed an accomplice who could understand the rollercoaster emotions and events that were occurring in her life, while at office she had submerged totally into her books which had given her the solace she wanted in a long time. As she was reading, she drifted into sleep not realizing the time her mother came and put a blanket on her and adjusted the room temperate while modulating the fan regulator, all the small gestures that could only indicate a mother's love.

Next morning, she woke up fresh and bright, her head feeling light on her shoulders, as she went along with her morning routine. She was getting ready for her job when she heard a small scoff and hustle coming from the kitchen. She quickly steadied herself and rushed to see if her mother was okay. She quickly observed her mother was in brawl with her cook, after much hustle she was able to calm her mother who had now turned red like a tomato because of her sudden fit of rage. After she was able to steady her mother and prepared an herbal tea to compose herself. Later she had dug the truth out of her mother and the words that came out of her mothers' mouth shocked her. It seemed that Tuesday 6th June which was 06 /06, Mrs Roy's cat had come under a track which was indeed 6666.Moreover, it had sent Mrs Roy into an utter shock and the whole neighborhood had to help her as she kept on howling for a week and went on uttering the sentence that, "*Maya the witch had cursed my son, she foretold the death of my son. I want that witch burnt.*"

The news of the misfortune event had spread like wildfire in the entire neighborhood and people started talking about it even though they tried to be discreet. The very next day the old cranky neighbor seemed to have fallen down the stairs and broken his lower part of the rib and his wife seemed to have spoken to the locality head who oversaw the neighborhood about the entire incident. She went on to say how Maya came and foretold her husband about the misfortunate event, Maya's mother was in disbelief that her daughter would be subjected to such instances, but Maya decided to confront her mother later that night or the next morning to avoid health disturbances.

That very night it was said that a very powerful geo storm also termed as *powerful meteor steroid shower* occurred which had changed the course of life instances for many as it had a very powerful impact on the astrological placements of many individuals. It is said during ancient times, the powerful sages in Hinduism could foretell the future events through the various astronomical and celestial events, meteor shower during specific timelines could have exclusive spiritual significance. Meteor asteroid shower during the pre-mercury retrograde, played a major role in many individuals lives. The same event was occurring during the current timeline, and this were triggering some people. After a while some people found this timeline to be healing and major events occurring during this time.

The next day the old neighbor's wife had visited, Maya's mother to compose herself knowing about her ill health. She also was quite worried about the ill-fitting rumors spread by people about a child, and this really worsened the situation. According to her, she knew all the events that occurred in the neighborhood were the result of some serious co- incidence. After the wife, had disappeared Maya decided to take her mother for an outing which would relax both of their nerves, so she booked movie tickets and planned an awesome lunch for both. Maya decided to tidy and dress herself to make herself feel better for the event. During the outing her mother felt relaxed and jovial especially as Chinese was her favorite cuisine. However, a specific event occurred during their lunch which both tried to avoid.

One of the restaurant staff was trying to handle various activities altogether, as there was shortage of staff. At one point Maya knew that he would be approaching the trolley which consisted of several stacked white plates, and it would have caused a major chaos with a gentle unintentional push from the staff and would have create a major brawl with his boss and a payment cut. Maya had foreseen all these events as she suddenly got up from the chair and pulled the staff member aside gently which aroused curiosity and queerness within him. Nothing went unnoticed in Maya's mothers' eyes she decided to avoid the topic to avoid disturbance in their peaceful schedule. As Maya and her mother were returning towards home, they found a small puppy dog which seemed new in the neighborhood and was roaming around cluelessly in search of its mother. She immediately knew what to do, she cradled the puppy in her small arms, the puppy was very cute and fell asleep immediately into her arms snuggling onto her chest like he found her long lost mother and was basking under its warmth. As she approached home, she quickly ordered a cute basket, with ribbons and a few chocolates. She immediately started penning down a poetry weaving around long-lost souls waiting to be united in heaven whilst angels were playing the flute and magical harps soothing the pain that had caused on the physical plane. While the puppy was in her house, she not only loved the puppy but milked it, sang a lullaby, and took the utmost care of. Sometimes, in the middle of the night, she covered the puppy in her doll's cloth and stroked his head whilst singing a moon light lullaby.

As her order approached her home, she carefully bathed him, tied a ribbon to his neck and around the basket and clothed the puppy in warm mini fleece blanket. She put her written poetry which was written on a handwoven paper and along with milk chocolates she advanced towards Mrs Roy's house. When she saw the porch was clearly dim lighted and the missing cat had created a vacuum and the usual chirpiness had been lost, even the birds which were usually perched on the local trees refused to sing as they could sense the loss and tears of Mrs Roy. She quickly placed the mini basket on the porch and started hiding behind the tree, to observe the domino effect of her recent activity.

After a few moments, the puppy started yelping sensing the sudden separation and started calling out for Maya. Mrs Roy suddenly appeared on the porch and started reading the letter while tears started rolling down her cheeks and after a long time, she realized that these tears were precious like emeralds as they emanated the sense of happiness around the environment. She quickly cradled the puppy around her arms and started weeping and kissed him on the cheek profoundly and christened him "*Chesire*" Slowly one of Maya's wishes were fulfilled, while she did feel relief at some point, but her heart was also heavy as she felt a sudden pang of pain because of the separation of the puppy which had formed a strong bond with the kid. She walked away, closed her eyes, and could feel the angels dedicating magical hymn towards her. As she was walking towards her home, she could feel the blurred images whirlpooling. She could foresee her mother dismissing the maid servant wanting to prepare a special meal for her daughter and she wanted to have the conversation with her daughter. Maya was prepared internally to have the conversation as she knew that time had come for her mother to know and be prepared for her gifted abilities. As she was straddling along and humming songs while returning home, she appeared to have visualized a strange yet lovable scene. The marigold bushes along the sidewalks had almost started emanating a fresh fragrant while singing to the song, ***"What's new pussycat,"*** knowing that the next entrant in her life would be of someone very special and meant for the long haul. Thus emerged the sweet kitty from behind the bushes which resembled Chesire.

"*Come to mummy*!" Maya smiled and cradled her into her arms, and the fragrant of marigold became stronger and stronger.

The cloud seemed to have taken a different shape and form whilst kitty was meowing. It was as if Hecates herself was blessing Maya to have discovered the deep magic within herself and acknowledge the power of same rather than being ashamed of it. Knowing Mahamaya would be one of the most successful magicians of the era and the world would have to put her on the altar rather than burn the ones like the ancient witch trials.

www.ingramcontent.com/pod-product-compliance
Ingram Content Group UK Ltd.
Pitfield, Milton Keynes, MK11 3LW, UK
UKHW041820200726
13854UKWH00001BA/142